TITCH J⌐

Titch Johnson wants to ⌐⌐⌐⌐⌐⌐ ⌐⌐ ⌐ᵣ being average and norma⌐ ⌐⌐ wants to be the best at some ⌐ᵣ he's not a champion runner like Mᵣ ⌐ᵣer Dixon and he doesn't have great ideas like Jarvis – the only thing he's any good at is balancing a fork on the end of his nose! As it turns out, though, this skill is not nearly as useless as it seems.

Mark Haddon is the author of a number of children's books, including *Gilbert's Gobstopper*, *A Narrow Escape for Princess Sharon* and *Gridzbi Spudvetch*. In addition, his illustrations and cartoons have appeared in leading newspapers and magazines.

Some other titles

Haddock 'n' Chips
by Linda Hoy

Harry and Chicken
by Dyan Sheldon

Harry the Explorer
by Dyan Sheldon

The Human Zoo
by Virginia Ironside

The Magic Skateboard
by Enid Richemont

Roseanne and the Magic Mirror
by Virginia Ironside

Stone Croc
by Penelope Farmer

The Summertime Santa
by Hugh Scott

TITCH JOHNSON,
ALMOST WORLD CHAMPION

MARK HADDON
Illustrations by
MARTIN BROWN

WALKER BOOKS
AND SUBSIDIARIES

LONDON • BOSTON • SYDNEY

This book is for Max,
when he is old enough to read it

First published 1993 by Walker Books Ltd
87 Vauxhall Walk, London SE11 5HJ

This edition published 1994

2 4 6 8 10 9 7 5 3

Guinness Publishing Ltd wish to state that they
no longer publish endurance records.

This book has been typeset in Plantin.

Printed in England by Clays Ltd, St Ives plc

British Library Cataloguing in Publication Data
A catalogue record for this book
is available from the British Library.

ISBN 0-7445-3175-6

Contents

Chapter 1

Not Everyone Can Be the Best

....

It had been a bad day at school for Titch.
Nothing had actually gone wrong – that
wasn't the problem. The problem was that it
had been such a *good* day for everyone else.

It started in assembly, when the headmaster
called his two best friends up on stage,
congratulated them and made the school give
them a round of applause.

First, it was Monster Dixon. He had just
won the County one hundred metres
championship. The headmaster said that
his performance was "splendid" and that he
was "a credit to the school".

Clap, clap, clap, clap.

Monster was a giant. He had legs like trees
and ran like a leopard in trainers. If you met
him, you might think he was stupid, because
he talked slowly and didn't say a lot. But he

wasn't stupid. He just didn't waste too much energy thinking or nattering. He had better things to do, like growing up to be an international athletics superstar.

Second, it was Jarvis. His dad worked as a doctor at the local hospital. The Special Care Baby Unit at the hospital needed money, so Jarvis had come up with the idea of holding a jumble sale at school to help raise it.

"Wonderful, wonderful," said the headmaster. "What an exceptionally good idea. You have my full support."

Clap, clap, clap, clap.

Jarvis was a short, round, freckled, posh boy, with ears that stuck out like wings. He wasn't really any brighter than Monster, but he talked so much and answered so many questions in class that he seemed a bit of a brain box.

Jarvis rather liked being short and round; so no one bothered teasing him about it. When he grew up, he was planning to be a film director or a banker or the owner of an airline – anything that meant he could have an enormous house with its own swimming pool.

All this congratulation was bugging Titch.

Why were other people so good at things? Why not him? He wanted to be good at things, too. He wanted to be special.
He didn't want to feel quite so ordinary.

He was a small boy with brown, mousy hair. He was sort of average at school.
He was sort of OK at sports. He lived in an ordinary sort of house. His dad was a postman and his mum worked behind the counter at a bank in town. They were really nice; but they were very, very normal.

Titch thought how good it would be if the headmaster called him up on stage in assembly one day. How this would happen, he didn't know. He couldn't run a hundred metres without stopping to get his breath back, and he never had wonderful, wonderful, exceptionally good ideas like jumble sales.

Yes, it was bugging him something rotten.

Later that evening, back in his bedroom, Titch was lying around on his bed doing the only thing he was really good at – balancing a fork on the end of his nose.

Not sideways; not the easy way. No, he was balancing it properly, with the handle on the tip of his nose and the prongs pointing straight up into the air. He'd been doing it for almost fifteen minutes now without it falling off.

It was a habit of his. The previous term he had trained himself to wiggle his ears. He had stood in front of the mirror, straining his muscles until his head ached. After eight weeks he had learnt to move his ears two or three millimetres. It wasn't very impressive.

The term before that, he had practised holding his breath for minutes at a time. This had just made him feel sick.

Balancing a fork on the end of his nose was a much better idea altogether. It didn't make him sick and he had turned out to be surprisingly good at it.

He had been balancing the fork for over half an hour now; without a wiggle, without a waver.

He tried to imagine the headmaster calling him up on stage to congratulate him for winning the County fork-balancing championship. It didn't seem very likely.

"Your supper's ready, love," said a voice.

It was Mum, who had just stuck her head round the door.

Titch jumped in surprise. The fork flew off his nose, spun high in the air, came down and stuck into his leg.

"Yee–ouch!"

Mum shook her head. "Honestly, Titch, you do play some silly games!"

Downstairs, Mum cleaned his leg and stuck a plaster over the three little red holes while Dad put supper on the table.

"Mum?" asked Titch.

"What, love?" she replied.

"Why can't I be good at something?"

"But you're good at lots of things," she answered. "You came seventh in maths. You're in the second football team. You almost got a prize for your geography project..."

"No," said Titch, "I mean really good. Why can't I be the best at something?"

"Not everyone can be the best," said Dad.

"It's not fair," moaned Titch. "The only thing I'm really good at is balancing a fork on the end of my nose."

"Well," said Dad, "perhaps when you grow up you will be the world champion fork balancer."

"Oh, great," said Titch.

"I think you still need some practice," laughed Mum, as she pressed the plaster down tight.

Chapter 2

Babies in Boxes

....

That weekend the jumble sale plan went into operation.

First stop was the hospital. Jarvis and Titch were going to visit the Special Care Baby Unit so that they could take photographs to stick on the jumble sale posters.

The two of them sat for ages in the waiting room. Titch balanced a Biro on his nose; and Jarvis fiddled with his camera. It was an extremely expensive Nikon 4500 FXZ something-or-other, which his parents had bought him for Christmas. He was taking a photograph of his shoes.

"It's fully automatic, see?" said Jarvis.

He pressed a button and a string of lights flashed on and off. It looked more like a spacecraft than a camera.

"Yeh," said Titch, taking the Biro off

his nose. "Brilliant."

It was typical of Jarvis. He loved showing off his latest toys. Titch didn't mind in the least. Jarvis seemed to get just as much fun from other people playing with them. You simply had to wait your turn and you'd soon be having a go yourself.

Jarvis took a photograph of the chair he was sitting on.

At last, a door opened and the two boys looked up. It was Dr Morton, Jarvis's father. He was freckled, too. He had the same enormous ears and he was even fatter than Jarvis; but he had more wrinkles, a white coat and a stethoscope poking from his jacket pocket.

"You can come in now," he said, "but you must promise to be very quiet."

"*Beep-tick-whirr!*" went Jarvis's camera.

Dr Morton frowned and Jarvis turned it off.

The two of them followed Dr Morton on to the ward. The floors were squeaky and the ceilings were white. All over the walls were pictures of clowns and bunnies and smiling frogs on lily-pads. Nurses hurried in and out and the air smelled of disinfectant.

Dr Morton led them into a little side room and said, "Here we are."

In front of them were seven babies. Each baby was lying inside a big plastic box that looked like a fish tank. The babies were covered in woollen mini-blankets and had little tubes going up their noses. There were bright lights inside the boxes and the babies were attached to machines that beeped and flashed continually.

"These are called incubators," explained Dr Morton. "We put sick babies inside them to help them get better. The incubators keep them warm and make it easier for them to breathe properly."

Jarvis put his camera to his eye, fiddled with a few knobs and took a photograph of an incubator with a tiny baby curled up inside.

"The problem is," continued Dr Morton,

"that we need more of them; and they are very, very expensive."

"Like a washing machine or a computer?" asked Titch.

"No," said Dr Morton, "not like a washing machine or a computer. More like a sports car. A very flashy sports car indeed."

"Oh," said Titch, amazed.

"We're going to have to sell a lot of jumble," said Jarvis.

"Indeed you are," Dr Morton agreed.

The following afternoon, Titch and Jarvis were lying around in Jarvis's bedroom. It was an enormous bedroom, because the Mortons were enormously rich. There was a radio-controlled car on the window sill. There was a TV and a video on the bedside table, and a plastic Wild West fort with over two hundred cavalry on the carpet. Titch wanted a room like this.

The two of them had just finished drawing up the poster for the jumble sale. It read:

And Jarvis's baby photograph was carefully
glued in the middle of the page.

Now that the poster was finished, Titch had
begun playing with the radio-controlled car.
He was zooming it round the carpet, skidding
it under the bed and crashing it into the Wild
West fort.

Jarvis was putting new stamps into his

album. The Mortons had relatives who lived all over the world, and whenever they sent letters Jarvis carefully peeled off the weird and wonderful stamps and stuck them into the album. That morning they had received a postcard from Jarvis's Uncle Bertram, who lived in Kenya.

"Just look at this!" exclaimed Jarvis.

Titch ran down a few more plastic cowboys, parked the car and wandered over. Jarvis was holding a huge, triangular orange stamp with a picture of a charging rhino on the front.

"It's so mega," said Jarvis, "it's just got to have a page all of its own."

That night, Titch lay dreaming of all the things he would have if his parents were rich. He would have a bedroom as big as a football pitch. He would have an electric go-kart and a track to race it on. He would have a stamp album three feet thick with a single, glorious stamp on every page.

Chapter 3

The Big Brainwave

A week later, Titch and Monster were standing in the school library. They'd come to help sort the jumble ready for the sale: old socks, fridges, umbrellas, stuffed parrots, radios, cricket bats – it all had to be arranged into piles.

They had been sorting, arranging and piling for twenty minutes when Monster suddenly shouted, "Gordon Bennett!"

Titch looked up and saw him taking a pair of trousers from a tatty bin bag and climbing into them.

"Huge, or what?" laughed Monster.

Titch laughed, too. Monster was big. Monster was bigger than most of the teachers. But the trousers came up to his armpits and bagged out round him like a circus tent.

"Who on earth did these belong to?" he asked. "He must have been gigantic!"

"Perhaps they belonged to two people," suggested Titch. He had walked across the room and was starting to climb into the trousers together with Monster. "Perhaps they were so poor they could only afford one pair between them."

By now Titch had climbed completely into the trousers and he and Monster were standing facing each other, leaning back on the waistband.

"I'll tell you a fact," said Monster.

Monster liked facts. His favourites were athletics records; but he knew plenty of others, too. He knew the height of the tallest building in the world. He knew the capitals of countries you'd never heard of. He knew how far it was to the moon, and the names of all the astronauts who'd been there.

"Go on, then," said Titch. "Tell me."

"The fattest man in the world was called Jon Minnoch," announced Monster. "He lived in America and he weighed over six hundred kilograms!"

"I don't believe you," scoffed Titch.

"It's true," replied Monster, "and I can prove it, too."

"OK," said Titch. "Prove it."

Together, wearing the one vast pair of trousers, they shuffled round the bookshelves until Monster was able to reach the *Guinness Book of Records* from one of the shelves. He took it down and flicked through the pages until he found what he was looking for.

"Here we are," he smiled, handing the open book to Titch.

Titch read the page in front of him. Monster had been telling the truth after all. In the centre of the page was a photograph of a man who was so big, it looked like he had been inflated with a football pump. Underneath the photograph, it said:

The Heaviest Human Being

The heaviest man in medical history was Jon Brower Minnoch of Bainbridge Island, Washington

State, U.S.A., who suffered from obesity from childhood. The 1.85 m former taxi-driver was taken into hospital in March 1978. It took a dozen firemen to move him from his home to a ferryboat. When he arrived at the hospital he was put into two beds lashed together. It took thirteen people just to roll him over. Doctors estimated that he must have weighed 635 kg.

"I wonder…" said Titch, who had already forgotten about Jon Brower Minnoch. "I wonder if there's a record for balancing a fork on the end of your nose."

"I don't know," said Monster, "but we can find out soon enough."

He turned to the back of the book and started running his finger down the index. There was a record for the largest sausage in the world (21 kilometres). There was a record for throwing an egg the furthest distance without breaking it (96.90 metres); and there was a record for running the hundred yards backwards (12.8 seconds). This last record impressed Monster a lot because it was only slightly slower than he could run it forwards.

But there was no record for balancing a fork on the end of your nose.

"You should write in," said Monster, "and claim the record."

"Nah," said Titch, "that's stupid."

Slowly Monster's face began to light up. "No," he said. "I've got an even better idea."

"What's that?" asked Titch.

"You do it for charity. You get people to sponsor you to balance a fork on the end of your nose and you raise money for the hospital."

"Maybe," said Titch, who wasn't at all sure about this.

But Monster had decided that the idea was a winner, and there was no stopping him.

"Listen. I'll be your trainer. We do it in the school gym. We get people in to watch and we get judges, and when you've done it we write in to the *Guinness Book of Records* and you become World Champion. It's a cinch."

Titch and Monster were still discussing the charity fork-balancing world record attempt, when Mrs Simpson, their form mistress, walked into the library.

"And how are you boys getting on sorting out all the –" she stopped suddenly. "What on earth are you doing?"

"We've got another brilliant plan for raising money," said Titch.

"That's wonderful," replied Mrs Simpson. "But why are you both wearing the same pair of trousers?"

Chapter 4

Titch in Training

Titch thought about Monster's idea. It had
sounded stupid at first; but the more he
thought about it the better it sounded.
After all, he *was* wonderfully, wonderfully,
exceptionally good at balancing a fork on
the end of his nose.

Yes, he decided, he'd go for it.

Before the week was over, Titch had got
everything organized. He'd written out
sponsor forms. He'd arranged to use the gym
on the afternoon of the jumble sale. He'd also
found two judges: Mrs Bale, the assistant
head, and Monster's dad. They would make
the whole thing official and ensure that there
was fair play.

"It sounds completely daft to me," said
Titch's dad, chuckling. "But seeing it's all in

a good cause…"

"You'll sponsor me?" asked Titch, handing him a form and a pen.

"Of course," he agreed, writing down his name. "Now, I seem to remember you're pretty good at this trick of yours, so how about twenty pence for every minute you keep it up?"

"Great!" said Titch.

"You can have the same from me, love," added his mum. "And we'll both be there, cheering you on, won't we, dear?"

"That we will," nodded Dad.

Mr Johnson, Titch's dad, knew how good Titch was at the balancing trick. Dr Morton, Jarvis's dad, hadn't a clue. When Titch took the sponsor forms round to his house, he was rather sniffy about the whole thing.

"Balancing a fork on the end of your nose?" He hooted with laughter. "That's impossible!"

"No, it's not," said Titch, feeling rather offended.

"It is," replied Dr Morton. "Look, even I can't do it."

He took a fork out of his kitchen drawer and tried balancing it on the end of his nose. Twenty times he balanced it. Twenty times it fell straight to the floor. He only gave up after he'd made a hole in his expensive shoes and nearly stabbed the dog.

"See what I mean?" he said. "I'll give you ten pounds if you can do it for a minute; and I doubt I'll lose my ten pounds."

"You'll sponsor me for ten pounds a minute?" asked Titch, holding his breath.

"OK," said Dr Morton, taking the form from Titch. "Though how you hope to raise any money like this, I really don't know."

Titch tried very hard not to cheer.

Dr Morton was in for a shock.

Titch was in training. Every evening after school, Titch and Monster went straight into Titch's bedroom for a practice session.

Carefully, Titch would sit down, breathe

deeply, relax, then put the fork on his nose; and it would stay there.

There wasn't a lot for Monster to do. Titch was in top form. The fork fell off only twice. Once when the cat leapt through the window and into Titch's lap. The other when a stray wasp stung Monster, making him scream so loudly that the neighbours came round to see what the matter was.

The day of the jumble sale drew rapidly nearer.

The school hall began to look like Aladdin's cave. Everyone seemed to be carrying old clothes and radiators and lampshades. There were piles of crockery and cardigans, plastic ducks and hatstands. Two mums had brought in home-made cakes to sell and Mr Beam, the maintenance man, had set up a coconut shy. Mrs Trout's recorder group were practising hard so that they could entertain everybody.

On Wednesday morning, in assembly, after

they'd finished the hymn, the headmaster stood up, thanked everyone for helping out, reminded them to bring their friends and families and was about to sit down again when he remembered something.

Beginning to chuckle quietly to himself, he said, "One more thing… I hear that David Johnson will be trying to balance a fork on the end of his nose tomorrow. Apparently, he is hoping to set some kind of world record. Do sponsor him if you can. I don't know whether he will raise any money or not, but I'm sure he will manage to keep people amused just by having a go."

At last Titch had had his name read out in assembly; except that it wasn't as he had imagined it. The headmaster thought the whole thing was a joke. And he had got Titch's name wrong, too. No one had called him David since he was three years old.

Chapter 5

Go For It!

··

When Titch and Monster arrived, the hall
was packed. A thousand people were fighting
over garden forks, egg cosies and second-
hand false teeth. The cakes were selling like
nobody's business and there was already a
long queue for the coconut shy. There was so
much noise, you could hardly hear Mrs
Trout's recorder group squeaking their way
through "Three Blind Mice". It was just as
well – they sounded awful.

Titch looked round the crowded room and
saw Mum and Dad standing next to a nearby
stall. They were deciding whether or not to
buy a furry, purple toilet-seat cover. Titch
crossed his fingers and hoped they decided
to spend their money on something else.
Catching his eye, they waved and abandoned
the toilet-seat cover to follow Titch and

Monster into the gym.

Titch was dressed properly for his world record attempt. Monster had wanted him to come in wearing a red silk jacket like boxers did when they came into the ring, but he couldn't find one at home. Instead, he was wearing his dad's dressing gown. Mum had stitched the words TITCH JOHNSON on the back in big yellow letters.

The gym was almost deserted. Jarvis was there, together with a few classmates. Mrs Simpson was there too, to give him moral support. Apart from that, there were only Titch's parents and the two judges, Mrs Bale and Inspector Dixon.

Inspector Dixon, Monster's dad, was enjoying himself immensely. He marched up to Titch and shook his hand.

"All set?" he said. "Right then, I'm looking forward to a good, clean competition with no cheating."

"Yes, sir!" agreed Titch, clicking the heels of his shoes together and slipping out of his dressing gown to reveal his T-shirt and tracksuit trousers.

"Can we see the fork, then?" said Inspector Dixon.

Titch handed it over, and the inspector inspected it.

"Looks fine to me," he announced, holding it above his head and demonstrating it to everyone. "No glue. No flattened end. All shipshape and Bristol fashion. What do you think, Mrs Bale?"

He handed her the fork; she checked it and finally handed it back to Titch.

With Monster at his side, Titch did a few stretching exercises and a couple of press-ups, then eased himself gently onto the competition chair. Carefully, coolly, he placed the handle of the fork on the end of his nose and nodded to Inspector Dixon. He was all set.

"On your marks ..." said Inspector Dixon, "get set ... go!"

Titch took his hand away from the fork and

Inspector Dixon pressed the button of his stopwatch.

"Go for it, champ!" said Monster, and the great Fund-Raising-World-Record-Breaking-Fork-Balancing-Attempt began.

The room began to fill up. Nobody had been particularly interested at first. They didn't want to see someone put a fork on his nose, only to see it fall straight off again, which was what they expected to happen. But when the fork had been balancing, steady as a rock, on Titch's nose for some twenty minutes or more, the news spread round the building like wildfire.

The coconut shy and the cake stall began to empty and people started crowding through the doors of the gym. Soon Titch was surrounded by a buzzing, jostling crowd.

"Quiet, please!" hushed Inspector Dixon. "Move back and give the young man some room!"

It was going like a dream. Monster

massaged Titch's neck like trainers are meant to do. Jarvis brought him cans of fizzy orange with straws in. His mum leaned close to his ear and said, "Looks like you're getting quite a fan club!" And his dad wandered round the audience, announcing proudly to everyone, "That's my young lad, that is."

Titch squinted out of the corner of his eye. All he could see were the heads, hundreds and hundreds of heads, all trying to get a glimpse of Titch Johnson, Fork-Balancer supreme.

It was more than two hours later when Dr Morton came into the gym. The room was jammed with people standing shoulder to shoulder and no one was saying a word. Inspector Dixon wouldn't let them.

Wondering what on earth was going on, Dr Morton squeezed his way through to the front, gazed at Titch in surprise and tapped Jarvis on the shoulder.

"Hi, Dad," said Jarvis.

"He's just started, has he?" asked the doctor.

"No," said Jarvis, "he's been going quite a while."

"Oh, right," said his dad. "Thirty seconds? A minute? Two minutes?"

"Two hours twenty-three minutes," said Jarvis, checking his watch.

Dr Morton's face went white. He was doing a sum inside his head. He'd agreed to pay Titch ten pounds for every minute he managed to balance the fork. Titch had been doing it for one hundred and forty-three minutes. Dr Morton already owed Titch one thousand four hundred and thirty pounds.

"Drop that fork!" he shouted, lunging towards Titch. "Drop it, now!"

"Hang on, sir," said Inspector Dixon, stepping smartly in front of him. "Step back please, or I shall have to arrest you for causing a disturbance."

Dr Morton staggered back into the crowd, covering his face with his hands.

"Don't worry about him," Jarvis said, bending close to Titch's ear and grinning. "He's got plenty of lolly."

Four hours into the record attempt, Titch started to panic. Balancing the fork was a doddle. The problem was the fizzy orange. It was hot in the gym and he'd finished four cans since he started. He desperately needed to go to the toilet. It wasn't something he'd thought about beforehand.

He mentioned it to Monster. Monster told Titch's mum. Titch's mum spoke to Inspector Dixon, and Inspector Dixon whispered with Mrs Bale.

Suddenly, when Titch thought he couldn't hold out any longer, Inspector Dixon climbed onto a table and ordered everyone out of the gym for five minutes. The room emptied, and the next thing Titch knew, he was being handed a large plastic jug.

"It's OK, love," said Mum. "We'll turn round."

Five hours into the record attempt, the headmaster came into the gym and personally congratulated Titch. Six hours into the attempt, people started to leave so that they could go home and have their suppers. Seven hours in, the caretaker came to lock up and was politely told to go away by Inspector Dixon.

Mum brought Titch his supper at ten o'clock. She chopped it into tiny, bite-sized pieces and dropped them, one by one, into his mouth. At eleven o'clock he cleaned his teeth, very carefully and very slowly.

At midnight, Jarvis fell asleep. At two o'clock in the morning, Mrs Bale fell asleep and had to be woken up because she was a judge. At three o'clock in the morning, Titch started to wobble. At four in the morning, he yawned, closed his eyes, fell flat on the floor and started snoring.

Chapter 6

Max Sucks His Thumb

It was the following afternoon and Titch was
lying on the lounge floor watching television.
He couldn't stand up on account of the
painful crick in his neck. When the reporter
from the *Hockley Herald* came round, Titch
had to be photographed lying on the sofa.
He didn't mind. For one thing, he had had
the day off school. For another, he was going
to be world champion.

"You were brilliant!" said someone behind
him.

Titch turned and saw Jarvis, who had
called round after school.

"Amazing!" agreed Monster, following him
into the room.

"So, how did the jumble sale go?" asked
Titch.

"It went really well," said Jarvis. "We raised over a thousand pounds."

"That's great," said Titch.

"Forget the jumble sale," laughed Monster. He was holding Titch's pile of sponsor forms. "Do you realize how much money *you* raised?"

"No," said Titch, "how much?"

"Ten thousand pounds."

"What?!" gasped Titch. He sat up in surprise, his neck twinged and he fell back on the floor again. "Ouch!"

"And half of that's from my dad," added Jarvis.

"Wow!" said Titch. "I mean, oh dear. That's a lot of money."

"Don't worry," Jarvis said. "He can find it somehow. He's loaded. Besides, I've told him that I don't mind having a very little present next Christmas."

Titch was soon surrounded by well-wishers. Mum and Dad came back from work; and shortly after them, Mrs Bale and Inspector Dixon appeared at the front door.

"Well done, love," said Mum, pecking him on the cheek.

"Bit of a star, eh?" added Dad.

"And soon to be the world record holder," said Inspector Dixon. "Mrs Bale and I have just written a letter to the *Guinness Book of Records* telling them all about your spectacular performance."

"If all goes well, you should be in next year's edition of the book," smiled Mrs Bale.

Titch looked up at the circle of faces above him and grinned from ear to ear.

So, the impossible happened. He got a round of applause in assembly after all – for balancing a fork on the end of his nose.

The headmaster, who had thought the idea so amusing only a week before, was now very impressed. When he announced how much money Titch had raised for the Special Care Baby Unit at the hospital, you could hear the five hundred pupils all gasping.

"I think that David Johnson deserves a very big round of applause," he announced.

Titch bowed and clapping exploded all round the room.

Titch enjoyed being called up on stage by the headmaster. But he enjoyed something else even more – and that was his trip to the hospital.

It was three weeks after his world record attempt. Dr Morton had grumbled and grouched about the money he had to pay out. But, finally, he had forgiven Titch for being so spectacularly good at balancing a fork on his nose and had written out a cheque for five thousand pounds. He had also invited Titch to the Baby Unit to see how they had used the money he had raised.

"Here it is!" announced Dr Morton.

They were standing in the same small room that he and Jarvis had stood in only weeks before. It still smelled of disinfectant, and there were still bunnies and frogs on the wall. But now there were eight plastic boxes instead of seven.

Dr Morton led him to the last incubator in the line and pointed. Inside was a tiny baby sleeping under a tiny pink blanket. On the front of the incubator was a plaque on which were the words:

PRESENTED TO THE HOSPITAL
WITH MONEY RAISED BY

TITCH JOHNSON.

Titch stared at the incubator and the baby and the plaque for a few minutes, then Dr Morton said, "There are some people here I'd like you to meet."

Titch looked up and saw two people he hadn't seen before, standing next to the incubator.

"Mr and Mrs Kingston," said Doctor Morton, introducing them. "That's Max, their baby, in your incubator."

Titch shook their hands and Mr Kingston said, "He's too small to be able to say anything, but if he could I'm sure he'd want to give you the most enormous 'thank you'."

Titch looked back at Max; but Max just smiled, shoved his thumb in his mouth and sucked.

Chapter 7

I Am Your Friend Alway

....

A week later, as Titch was getting ready for school, Dad came into the kitchen with the post and said, "There's something for you. Looks very official."

Titch took a mouthful of toast and jam and cut open the long white envelope with his buttery knife. Inside was a typed letter which read:

2nd August 1991

<u>Guiness Book of Records</u>
Guiness Publishing Limited
33 London Road
Enfield
Middlesex EN2 6DJ

Dear Mr Johnson,

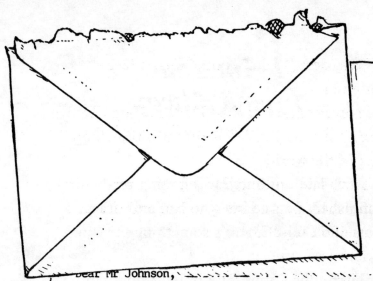

Dear Mr Johnson,

We were very interested to hear of your
attempt to set a world record for balancing
a fork on the end of your nose. Unfortunately,
I have to tell you that last month, Mr Carlos
Estevas, who lives in Guatemala in Central
America, set a world record of two days, five
hours, nine minutes and forty-six seconds.
I realize that this must be very disappointing
for you, and I'm sorry that you have been
so unlucky.

Yours sincerely,

Reginald Haversack

MR REGINALD HAVERSACK

"Oh, dear," said Mum. "That's really rotten luck."

"Never mind," smiled Dad, ruffling Titch's hair. "At least you know that you're second best in the world."

Titch said nothing. He left his toast unfinished, packed his gym bag and dragged himself off to school.

It was nearly a month later that something even stranger came for him in the post. Dad dropped the parcel next to Titch's cereal bowl and said, "Why don't *I* ever get anything this interesting?"

Titch put down his spoon and stared at the package. The postmark said ANTIGUA, GUATEMALA. There were so many stamps on it, there was hardly space for Titch's address. On the stamps were pictures of parrots and aeroplanes, panthers, pyramids and jungles, all in vivid colours. He opened it carefully so as not to tear any of them. Inside there was a letter:

My Most Dear Mr Titch,

Please do excuse my Inglish. I read the newspapers in Inglish but do not it speek much. My name is called Carlos Estevas. I have world record for keeping fork on nose. But I read in newspaper that you keep fork on nose for 12 hour. And you very little. This is good. I congratulating you, and sending you present of my fork I use. Keep trying, then maybe you beat me one day some time.
Much Luck.

I am your friend alway,

Carlos Estevas.

Titch unwrapped the rest of the parcel. Inside was a battered old fork, which had been nailed to a flat piece of wood and put inside a brightly painted picture frame. There was also a signed photograph of Mr Estevas standing outside his house.

Titch took the thirty-four stamps off the parcel and managed not to tear any of them. Every single one was different. He found an empty photograph album in the cupboard under the stairs and carefully stuck a single stamp in the middle of each huge white page.

That night, Titch flicked through the album as he lay in bed before going to sleep. Then he looked up at the photograph of Mr Estevas he had pinned to his wall beside the framed fork. Mr Estevas was standing next to a little stone house, wearing a floppy straw hat. Behind him, children were playing, chickens were scratching and an old lady was dozing happily in a hammock. Far in the background were high blue mountains that looked like something out of a fairy tale.

Titch closed his eyes and started to drift off to sleep. He thought about Max, the little baby sleeping in the incubator with his own name on the side. He hoped he would get better soon and go home to his mum and dad.

Yes, it was all right. He didn't mind being second best in the world.